THE SO-SO CAT

by EDITH THACHER HURD
Pictures by CLEMENT HURD

HARPER & ROW, Publishers • New York, Evanston, and London

THE SO-SO CAT
by Edith Thacher Hurd, Pictures by Clement Hurd
Printed in Switzerland for Harper & Row, Publishers, Incorporated, 1964
All rights reserved
For information address Harper & Row, Publishers, Incorporated
49 East 33rd Street, New York 16, N. Y.
Library of Congress Catalog Card Number: 64-19608

THE SO-SO CAT

Once upon a time in a faraway land where the wind howled all the time, there lived a cat so big and so, so black that he was called the So-So Cat.

The So-So Cat lived with a witch and two timid owls in the top of a tall, tall tree.

On the outside the house looked like a lump of leaves, a bunch of mistletoe, or a thing in the top of the tree.

But on the inside the house was filled with cozy things, things that cats and owls and witches like: dead mice, old cheese, bottles, books on magic, masks and mysterious noises all around.

Now the So-So Cat, the witch, and the two timid owls should have been very happy in the cozy house but they were not because the witch was a woman full of plots and plans. She knew a thousand spells and she was always casting one about her.

Sometimes at night she put on her hat, waved her wand, and made the owls and cat ride away on the wind with her.

Sometimes she changed the owls to mice.

But worst of all, she sometimes turned the So-So Cat into a rat. How do you think a big black cat would like a thing like that? Not much.

So one dark night when the wind was blowing a gale outside and the witch was busy dreaming dreadful dreams, the cat went off with the witch's hat. He took her wand. He carried away her broomstick. And he hid them all in a hiding place that only he could find.

"I'll leave them there till Halloween," he said. "For hats and wands and witches' sticks are not for everyday."

The very next night when the witch had finished putting away the dirty dinner dishes, which she never washed, she rubbed her bony hands together. She rattled her rumbly voice and muttered:

> *Broomstick, broomstick in the air,*
> *Keep us flying everywhere.*
> *In the darkness of the night,*
> *Dreadful things are my delight.*
> *So let us neither stop nor stay,*
> *Until we see another day.*

When the witch had finished casting her spell about, she looked around for her wand. But she could not find it anywhere.

"Where is my wand?" the old witch cried.

"Oh, oh, we don't know," hooted the two owls timidly.

"And I don't care," replied the cat, and that made the witch very angry.

The two little owls looked high and low. They looked everywhere that they could think of: underneath the old dead mice, behind some moldy cheeses, inside of all the bottles. But of course they could not find the witch's wand.

Only the So-So Cat knew where it was and he was curled before the fire, purring happily.

The next night when the witch finished putting away the dirty dinner dishes, she said to the cat and the owls, "You stay here and take care of the house, for I am going out to find my wand."

With that she put on her shawl and her big rubber boots, but she could not find her hat.

"The rain is raining cats and dogs. The wind is blowing a gale again, so how can I go out without my hat?" the witch said angrily.

"Oh, oh, we don't know," hooted the two owls timidly.

"You can't," said the cat, and then he went back to sleep again.

Now the witch was beginning to worry, for what is a witch without a hat and what is a witch without a wand on Halloween?

The next night the witch did not even wait to put away the dirty dinner dishes.

"Don't expect me home till late," she said. "I'm going out to search all night and hunt all day until I find my hat and wand."

With that she opened the door of the house in the top of the tall, tall tree and was just about to step out, when the two tiny owls hooted: "Oh, oh, oh, look out! Look OUT! You haven't got your broomstick!"

The witch stopped quickly. She slammed the door hurriedly. And sure enough, she didn't have her broomstick.

And what would happen to an old witch who stepped out of a house in the top of a tall, tall tree without her broomstick? Well, just about the same thing as would happen to you or me, only it would happen to us even if we did have a broomstick.

The old witch trembled like a leaf in the wind. She was beside herself with fear. What a terrible thing had almost happened to her. She sat down in her rocking chair and rocked and rocked. The owls brought hot tea to comfort her.

Then all of a sudden the witch let out an awful scream. "Where IS my broomstick?" she cried.

The So-So Cat just opened an eye from where he lay before the fire, but the two timid owls were already looking everywhere.

From that day on, the witch hardly moved from her chair. All day she spent rocking and thinking. Where have my wand and my hat and my broomstick gone? Where, oh, where can they be?

Halloween was coming faster than ever. The days were just flying by: Monday, Tuesday, Wednesday, Thursday, Friday.

Saturday was Halloween!

Halloween morning dawned bright and clear. The witch looked at the calendar that hung on the wall by the chimney place. Sure enough, it would be full moon that night.

"Just perfect for broomstick riding," sighed the witch, "and I look so well on mine. Everybody says so."

When darkness came at last and the sun sank into the west, pumpkins began to go on everywhere. There were pumpkins smiling happily. The witch didn't think much of that kind of pumpkin. There were pumpkins with leery, sneery, growling grins, and that was the kind the witch liked best.

The moon crept over the hill and into the trees beyond. It stretched itself over the land in black and yellow shadows.

The witch looked out of her house in the tall, tall tree. She saw all the other witches practicing with their wands and muttering magic spells and phrases. She could see them brushing the dust from the brims of their hats and trying them on in their mirrors. A broomstick hung by every door, polished and shiny and ready.

"Oh," the old witch wailed, "what
is a witch without a stick? I can't go out
without my hat. The snakes and rats,
the beetles and bats won't pay any atten-
tion to a poor old witch without a wand."

"That's right," said the So-So Cat as
he moved off the mat before the fire. He
stretched his long sleek back. He bristled
up his whiskers. He curved his tail to look
like a hook and disappeared into the moonlight.

22

The So-So Cat went out to get the witch's hat. He went out to get her wand and broomstick. But when he came to the secret place where he had hidden the witch's things, there was no hat, no wand, not even the witch's broomstick.

The cat looked here. He looked there. Then he began to worry. The night was passing fast. Halloween would soon be over.

He looked in every nook and cranny. He hunted in every tumbled stump and searched in caves and haunted houses, but he could not find the witch's hat. He could not find her wand or broomstick.

Then all of a sudden from a tiny shadow something spoke to the So-So Cat.

"I'm looking for a cat," it said, "and you are so, so big and so, so black, will you be MY big black cat?"

Out of the tiny shadow stepped a tiny witch. She wore a great big hat. She carried a great big wand and she was trying to ride on a grown-up's broomstick.

"I have a witch," the cat replied. "But she's always casting spells about and she's often cross and cranky."

"Then ride with me," said the little witch. "I'm always very kind and good, only sometimes cross and cranky."

So the So-So Cat jumped onto the back of the tiny witch's broomstick. He waited for her to wave her wand. He waited for her to cast a spell.

But the little witch didn't say a word and ABSO-LUTELY NOTHING happened!

"Quick," said the cat. "Wave your wand. Cast a spell and let's be off, for the night is passing fast and Hallow-een will soon be over."

"I don't know how to cast a spell," said the tiny witch unhappily. "I don't know a single magic word or any magic phrases."

"Then where did you get that hat?" said the cat. "Where did you get that great big wand? And where did your broomstick come from?"

"They came from the wind," said the little witch. "The wind blew them into my yard one night, and I found them there in the morning."

"They are not yours," said the So-So Cat.

"Yes, they are," said the little witch. "The wind blew them into my yard and they are MY Halloween costume."

"But you don't know any magic," said the cat. "You don't have any plots or plans. You do not know how to cast a spell."

"No," said the little witch. "But I could learn to."

"I don't think so," said the cat. "So give me your hat and stick and wand and leave witches' work to witches."

"I won't. I won't. I won't!" cried the little witch. "They are MY Halloween costume and I am going to wear them."

"No," said the cat. "They are NOT your Halloween costume, for I know which witch they belong to and she is full of plots and plans. She knows a thousand spells."

But still the little witch would not give up the costume, until at last the cat said softly, "If you will give me your Halloween costume, MY witch will give you another."

"But how?" said the little witch.

"Didn't I tell you to leave witches' work to witches?" said the cat.

"But will you come back?" said the little witch as she took off the witch's hat.

"I'll do the best I can," said the So-So Cat.

Then he took the hat, the wand, and the broomstick and disappeared into the moonlight.

The **old** witch could hardly believe her eyes when she saw what the cat had brought her. He told her where he'd found her things and he told her what he'd promised.

The old witch rubbed her bony hands together. She rattled her rumbling voice. Then quick as a wink, without stopping to think, she rushed to the window and cast a spell in the moonlight.

Choose whatever you like best.
My trusty wand will do the rest.
Be a cat or be a rat.
Be a witch in a witch's hat.
Be a ghost all dressed in white,
Scaring people in the night.
Be a pumpkin, round and fat.
Be a scary little bat.
Choose whatever you like best.
My trusty wand will do the rest.

30

When the witch had finished, she waved her wand in the air three times to make the spell come true.

"Now," she said, "are we ready, my owls and you bad black cat?"

She tucked her hair up under her hat. She flung her leg astride of her broomstick. She waved her wand in the air and began to chant: "Broomstick, broomstick in the air..."

But long before the old witch could finish the spell, a very small witch, on a brand new broomstick, flew away with the So-So Cat.